A Seed Falls on Okinawa

A Soldier's Story

Peter A. Hewett

Copyright ©1949 - 2012 Peter A. Hewett

Newly edited and rereleased by AnEx Publications 2012

First Paperback Edition - 2012

ISBN 978-0-9711774-5-1

LCCN: 2012915230

anexpublications.com

PRINTED IN THE UNITED STATES OF AMERICA

THERE WERE NO ATHEISTS IN THE FOXHOLES

DEDICATION

Dedicated to:

The late Frederick J. Eichhorn, Jr.

Grand Knight, Council #67, Knights of Columbus - Lawrence, MA
"His unflagging devotion to the principles of charity, unity, fraternity and patriotism should serve as a shining example to those who strive to foster the virtues he espoused."

ACKNOWLEDGMENTS

The author wishes to express his deepest gratitude to the following:

Mr. James F. Hennessey
Superintendent of Schools Lawrence, Massachusetts
Mr. Joseph T. Harty
Worthy Grand Knight, - Lawrence Council #67
Knights of Columbus
Mr. Francis X. Hogan
Director, Lawrence Industrial School
Lawrence, Massachusetts

And also to those numerous others whose enthusiastic cooperation
and wise counsel made the writing and publication of this story
possible.

Cover photo: Marine Corporal Earl Brunitt (left) and Private
Genare Nuzzi share a foxhole on Okinawa with a war orphan,
April 1945. Photographed by Sgt. W.A. McBride or Sgt. Howard
S. England, (U.S. Marine Corps); this public domain photo is free
of known restrictions under copyright law, including all related and
neighboring rights. NARA (National Archives and Record
Administration FILE #: 1127-N-118933 WAR & CONFLICT
BOOK #: 881

NOTE:

"What really happened on Okinawa cannot be reported in the photographs or the brief outline of 'One Year.' "The picture of a bleak cliff here might appear as just a cliff, but whatever occurred there may be written in histories to be read by generations of the future. And the experiences of the men who crouched in foxholes at that cliff may fill novels in the literature of the future."

The above quotation is from a souvenir booklet entitled, ""One Year", April 1, 1945 - April 1, 1946". Edited by The Public Relations Office, Okinawa Base Command. Sponsored by The Army Exchange Service, Printed and published by Kelly and Walsh, Ltd., Shanghai.

"A Seed Falls on Okinawa" is one writer's humble contribution to the "literature of the future" first envisioned by the officers who produced that booklet.

CONTENTS

FORWARD

This is the story of a seed—a seed that died as all seeds must die in order that a plant may be born. It is the story of a tree — no — the story of three trees — a trinity of trees: the mustard tree spoken of in the Gospel, a pine tree on Okinawa and the Tree of the Cross. Trees and the trinity — we think we see three, in reality we see only one. Trees have a great fascination for all of us whether they are Kilmer's, the family, Brooklyn's or Eden's. Who would deny that Eden's and Brooklyn's trees have much in common? Or that our family tree and Kilmer's are of the same mold? "Only God can make a tree."

Seeds and plants and trees — he who plants knows that cultivation must follow and after cultivation the flowering, the blooming and later the harvest.

This story lets us in at the planting — we are enthralled at the cultivation and impatient for the harvest. Indeed "a seed must die" that somewhere, something must live.

Rev. John J. Lamond, O.S.A

PROLOGUE

It all began so very, very long ago; back before the stirring days which followed when a Japanese Sea and Air Task Force stealthily crossed the Pacific Ocean early on a Sunday morning, unleashing a sudden, unwarranted attack upon The United States military installations at Pearl Harbor.

Yes, it was long ago and far away in that distant period when we bathed in blissful ignorance. As a nation, we lived like children; with a phantom Pied Piper, luring us with his ever-beckoning finger toward the all too realistic borderline of Maturity.

The year was 1918. The first phase of a world-wide struggle of diverse ideologies which would re-erupt in flaming fury twenty-one years later had just been brought to a close. Factory whistles and fire-bells competed with each other in their screeching and clanging reverberations. The hysterical repercussions served only as a staged background for a small gathering of typically American kids who patriotically paraded up and down an unpaved hillside street, laboriously expending their energies by beating upon old wash tubs, dish pans and assorted kitchenware.

Blending into the rising crescendo of elated gaiety and relief, the lusty but barely audible faint cries of a newly born infant in a nearby house joined with the jubilant yells of the celebrating youngsters in the street. The young mother of the child stood bending over the bassinet in a contemplative manner and silently breathed a prayer for both her own and a world's deliverance from pain, much like another Mother over nineteen centuries before.

Outside in the yard, shining in the gloss of its painted surface, stood an attractive bobsled, fashioned by the skilled hands of this tiny baby boy's father.

It was Armistice Day, 1918. The war to end all wars had ended. Coincidentally, a spectacular period of glorious boyhood had also drawn to a dramatic close. No more would the nearby woods and fields resound to the valiant battle cries of the simulated warfare which for months past had surged back and forth over unbloodied ground.

A few years passed. Another Armistice Day, sober and solemn, was dutifully observed as a frigid winter set in too early that season. Blustery storms blanketed the green earth with a heavy white cover. Every day saw the hillside street filled with young coasters who rode their sleds down the steep incline, wind whipping their cheeks as they skillfully maneuvered the steel runnered sleds over the icy road.

The star-studded nights, crisp and cold, served to add further to the zestful enjoyment of a particular group, one of whom owned the long-planked bobsled capable of seating six or seven passengers. The little fellow who's Dad had built the sled always took his rightful place behind the steering wheel, salvaged from an old Tin Lizzie.

Coasting, bobsledding, skating, snow fighting and skiing comprised the necessary exertions that added height and weight to these prospective men of the future.

Spring arrived. The newly turned furrows, awaiting only the dropping of the seed, gave promise of numerous "spud roasts" later in the year to these youngsters who always returned home after such feasts to their dismayed mothers looking like end men in an all star minstrel show.

The neighborhood resounded to the crack of a baseball bat; to a speeding runner striving to stretch the hit into a triple; to the umpire's call of "you're out," and finally to the divisive squabble which inevitably followed.

After weeks of prolonged impatience, schools closed for summer vacation. Lazy days stretched far ahead into golden September. Days that held forth promises of campfires beside a meadow brook; of climbing trees to see who could ascend to the topmost branches; days of romping across fields with a companionable dog; of lying upon the warm, soft earth, gazing up into the blueness of infinity and comparing the rolling cloud formations to fairy castles or listening to the raucous cawing of the recently returned crows.

Over the crest of the hillside street where boys played "Duck on the Rock", "Relievio" or "Long-horse", lay the vast, landed estate of a baronial millionaire. The confines of the immense acreage were guarded by high stone walls erected at tremendous cost to satisfy the eccentric whims of the owner. Within this sacrosanct area stood an old abandoned dwelling, which, because of its dilapidated condition, the mysterious idiosyncrasies of its master, and the tales which were retold concerning him, was known as "the haunted house". To pass by the haunted house at any time required all the courage that any little boy was capable of mustering.

The play-filled seasons rolled in their exact succession like well ordered factories turning out the products of the passing years. Boyhood and its joys moved into the past without even a reluctant, backward glance. - Willing hands dutifully grasped the torch.

PART ONE
THE SOWING

He was numb-tired. Crouching low in the foxhole, sleep for him had been a matter of fitful snatches of nerve twitching unreality during which he had lain for hours while he and the outpost detachment had held off the probing thrusts of Japanese infiltration. Banzai attacks during the day were nerve-shattering and inconceivable to his western mind, but somehow he felt capable of defending against these fanatical attacks. It was the night he most feared; it was the night which held the most suspenseful terrors.

Thoroughly indoctrinated he had been; yet still he wondered about the underlying reasons for the world-shattering events and circumstances which had caused him and all the others to find themselves holed up in spaded excavations; dug deep on a foreign, godforsaken island ten thousand miles from home.

Home! The fleeting thought of the word and all that it implied excited an entirely new train of thought. The shifting scenes of memory flashed rapidly as he reviewed past events and youthful aspirations.

Strange that tonight of all nights his mind should dwell so persistently on all that he had left behind. Certainly, there hadn't been a day or a night that he didn't think of home ever since the moment he had departed for boot camp.

Those thoughts had prompted the normal correspondence routine; coupling filial duty to his parents and social obligations to his friends. The letters had been the usual type: his first impression of life in the service; its newness and completely abrupt change from civilian status; all the joys and pleasures of newly-formed companionships; and of course, the gripes when he found things particularly irksome, especially when compelled by discipline to conform to the rigid pattern of military routine.

Yes! There was something about this very night that was distinctly different. Somehow, the stars seemed closer than usual, as if one had only to reach up and pluck a bright, gleaming diamond from the sky. He marveled mutely at the magnitude of the universe. Yet, in some unexplainable manner, God seemed so very near tonight.

Here in the solitude of the enveloping darkness he found himself prey to the same type of uneasiness he had completely forgotten, but which tortured him back in his childhood days when his mother had closed the door leaving him alone in an unlit room.

All about was the quiet of night, its stillness to his ears broken only by the buzzing of the mosquitoes around him, while in the trees above, the locusts droned ceaselessly in a maddening symphony.

No man, friend or enemy, dared to change his position in the foxholes, lest the mere crackling of a bone joint, stiffened by immovability, should betray the presence of the body and the person to which it was attached.

"When I was a kid" — nostalgically he half whispered the preliminary phrase which invariably antecedes the narration of some happy anecdote connected with that fleeting period. Vivid and clear, the acute pictures impressed years before upon the retentive imagery of his alert, young mind rolled out before him as if on a movie screen.

It had been a terrifically hot day in June, he recalled. He and his lusty, barefooted companions, conspirators in many an escapade of deviltry sauntered idly and unhurriedly down a dusty, country lane leading to a small swimming pond which afforded complete sanctuary to the cult of those who sought escape from the persecutions of misunderstanding parents, diabolically intent upon their enslavement by the mowing of lawns, running of errands, washing of dishes, unquestioned and immediate obedience and the numerous other entrapments of civilization.

Now and then they paused at some familiar trysting place to search for fallen coins, lost from the side pockets of heedless swains, more intent upon their romancing than the preservation of their currency.

These spots were, of course, regarded as secret and exclusive by moon-struck sweethearts, but were never quite secluded enough to escape the knowledge and the prying, inquisitive eyes of curious imps of mischief. On innumerable occasions, young couples, resting on a grassy knoll after strolling down lovers lane had had their reveries and hand-holding dreams of rose-entwined cottages rudely interrupted by the sudden, whooping onslaughts of these small fry who were lacking in both regard and understanding of the lover's way.

These interlopers were wont to edge their creeping and belly-sliding approach through the undergrowth, with the lovers oblivious and unaware of their stealthy closeness until the moment of the seemingly fanatical attack where they would rise up screeching, "Kiss her! Kiss her!" at the top of their vigorous, young lungs, overrunning Cupid's citadel and disappearing into the early dusk of night, their gleeful laughing fading gradually as they fled in fear of indignant reprisal.

Now, under a hot daytime sun, their painstaking and thorough search of the area for lost coins had been unrewarded. Relinquishing the task with the shoulder- shrugging attitude of their years, they resumed their ambling gait down the road. Then cutting off into the woods, they followed a zigzag path in single file, Indian fashion, drinking in the zestful, life-sustaining odors of pine-pitch, wild flowers, rotting logs and finally, the dank smell of the shore-line vegetation which bespeaks the nearness of water.

Young boys have been so aptly described as a blended

combination of the various animals that they unconsciously imitate. The sight of the inviting waters caused them to alert like startled fawns at the signal of impending danger; to break into a bounding, scrambling run, leaping rabbit-like over logs and rocks, meanwhile hauling and tugging in an "on the run" effort to divest themselves of recalcitrant, sweat-stuck shirts.

Huffing and puffing upon arrival at the shore's edge saw them excitedly peeling off their trousers in a fumbling, over-exerted endeavor to maintain the boyish prestige of being the "first one in."

The practically simultaneous splashes reverberated throughout the woods as their tanned and lithesome bodies disappeared beneath the surface only to emerge in a moment, spurting water in elongated, curving trajectories and with an indiscriminate selection of target adversaries. Submerging and resurfacing, they rolled and dodged in desperate attempts to escape the bewildering streams, which reminded him so much now of the efficiency of the deadly flame-throwers in use against the stubborn obstinacy of Japanese resistance.

The sound of a shell exploding in the distance brought his mind back to the present. That idyllic day suddenly seemed so far away, so unreachable. It was a phase of his life and that of every normal boy, which, having once passed, can never be recaptured. Happy, carefree days of childish irresponsibility and uninhibited abandon! How he wished he could just close his eyes and awaken back on that day.

Later, tired with swimming, he and a couple of his friends lounged indifferently on the yielding cushion of the grass-blown bank. Their conversation concerned the newly-healed appendectomy scar, livid and red, slashing across the abdomen of one who took justifiable pride in its possession to the exclusion of all the others. Not a single one of them could lay claim to such distinction.

"Yes sir," the kid exclaimed. "This is one of the longest scars my doctor ever had to make because my appendix was abscessed." . . . He nodded affirmatively by way of emphasis. He went on, "Not only that, fellers, but it ruptured and the doctor had to work real fast before the poison traveled through my system."

He looked at his listeners and with a determined air, added, "Someday, when I grow up, I'm going to be a doctor too, and help save people from having poison go through their systems."

"Yeah, go'wan," another kid jeered. "Who wants to be an ol' doctor tending a bunch of fussy old ladies?" When there was no response, he continued, "I'm gonna be a fisherman on a big boat and sail out to sea where the waves are rough and sometimes you have to go to the help of sinking vessels and the rescue of. . . ." He paused gropingly for the right phrase to use and then, his face aglow with the success of his effort he finished the sentence, "Fair damsels in distress." He too, beamed conclusively.

The boy in the foxhole reflected that he had listened to both of them in silence, his attention, at that moment, drawn somewhat musingly to the several occupants of two log rafts which floated a short distance from shore. On one of the rafts, two boys were occupied in casting worm-baited, lead-sinkered, fishing lines, swinging the weighted twine around and around their heads before releasing them in a long throw far out into the center of the pond. Laboriously, they pulled the lines back to the raft. Re-examining and adjusting the wriggling bait with expert eyes, and with the untiring diligence of those who pursue this fascinating avocation, they patiently cast and recast the continually fishless lines.

He lay there on the bank in almost the same position he now occupied in the foxhole. They had turned to him and almost in unison had asked, "What are you gonna be?"

Again he visualized the crystalline scene, and recalled his reply and all that it meant for him today: the passing years, the long nights of grinding home-work for school; and now, here in an entrenched foxhole, patiently waiting for the dawn of another day.

He heaved a sighing shrug of resignation to the destinies his road of life had taken. Across the years he remembered his exact reply as though the thought had been voiced only a moment before.

He said, "I'm gonna be both a doctor and a fisherman!" "What d'ya mean?" they exclaimed, "Yah can't be both!"

"Oh, yes I can," he insisted. "I'm gonna be a doctor to help keep poison from going through people's minds and a fisherman to catch men in order to save their souls"

He paused momentarily and then half-sheepishly, pulled the trigger for the second time of his double-barreled, pent-up, emotional ambitions.

He said, "I'm gonna be a Missionary in faraway places to spread the teachings of Jesus." They looked at him in wide-eyed amazement. He had been a clean-minded kid and from the time they were toddlers, had always merited the respect of "the gang."

"Gee, yeah," they reiterated as one remarked, "You'll really make one hell of a missionary!"

Then, on that same night, after evening prayers had been said at his mother's knee, he looked up into her face, repeating the conversation of the afternoon.

"Do ya know what they said, Ma?" he inquired.

"No, son, what?" she asked.

"They said, I'd make one hell of a missionary."

She laid a hand upon the head .of the pint-sized figure kneeling before her, sudden tears rimming her eyes but forcibly held back lest he perceive the welling over of her emotions. In a soft tone of voice she said, "Only if it is God's will, do you understand?"

"Yes, Mother" he replied, "I understand."

His nostalgic recollections once again ended abruptly. A machine gun chattered somewhere over to his left and instinctively he lowered his head, compressing the muscles of his neck. For a few moments, he dared not make a single other move. Following the sequence of his thoughts, however, he reached cautiously into an upper pocket of his combat jacket and withdrew a small silver crucifix which he reverently pressed to his lips. A small silver crucifix.

The carbine lay at an angle across his thighs. His trigger finger was loose in the grip. In his left hand, he clenched the crucifix. Tense and alert, every fiber of his being attuned for an immediate emergency, he sweated out the endless eternity of the night.

Now, instinctively he went over the instructions and orders the patrol had received regarding the desirability of taking prisoners for purposes of interrogation. Headquarters was in dire need of knowledge concerning the unit identifications, dispositions and strength of the enemy.

He knew the routine. He had had his fill of theoretical practice and repetitive drilling from the day he had taken the oath as a callow, slope-shouldered recruit to the time he emerged from boot camp, as a robust, filled out, well-knitted specimen of The United States Marine Corps.

Yes, and he had had enough of actual practice also. "Merciful God," he intoned to himself, "Is there no end to these islands that keep stretching ever northward?"

Now he peered strainingly into the impenetrable darkness.

"The naval barrage should start anytime now," he reflected. How eagerly he looked forward each night to the heartening and morale-boosting effect of the heavy guns of the task force that stood off-shore and poured its cannonades into the enemy positions. Particularly, he awaited with hushed expectancy for the arrival of the star shells, bursting high in the air and illuminating the surrounding scene in a bright light reminiscent of the fireworks displays back home. The thought stirred him to a sense of comparative and relaxed satisfaction. He held the crucifix lightly in his hand.

"Strange," he thought, "how a light can dispel the gloom and sense of loneliness."

Like a thunderclap announcing the unsuspected arrival of a midsummer storm, the naval barrage burst forth with a crushing fury. Explosion after explosion rocked the Japanese front and rear positions. A star shell broke into thousands of fragments of streaming wide-spreading phosphorescence. Night turned to day.

It was at that identical moment that he saw the Jap soldier's face at the very brink of his foxhole. The Jap held a knife between tightly clenched teeth. Another six inches forward and he would tumble into the occupied slit.

Both were shocked and startled at the mutual discovery but his reactions were quicker and faster than the Jap's. Leaping up, he slid his left hand around the back of his adversary's neck and with his other hand under the enemy chin, he twisted his head, and pulled the slight figure into the foxhole, belly down. Without hesitation, he pinioned the Jap's arms from behind while digging his knee into the small of the little man's back.

It had happened in an instant of time. All tight inside, sweat oozing from his pores; legs quivering from the fear and exertion; his heart beating wildly and thumping against his ribs; lips compressed into a grim line of muscle, tight with determination to hold his prisoner, he exhaled his constricted breath through widely dilated nostrils. "I've caught one," he exulted inwardly, "I've caught one".

The last faint glow of the fading star shell glimmered lingeringly when just at the instant of its final extinction, the retaliatory mortar fire of a Japanese battery opened up. The first shell, describing the high arc of its curving line of flight, burst with a resounding roar directly over the foxhole.

In that split second of nebulous surprise, he saw thousands of multi-colored orbs floating hazily afar in space. Despite his closed eyelids, he distinctly saw them converge into a single but gigantic sphere of luminous, yet deliciously comforting softness.

Night, ever an indulgent mother, pulled the cover of her darkness like a sheltering cloak of black velvet over the foxhole. Both sides ceased firing. All again was deathly still and silent in the misty, chilling damp of that Okinawa valley.

PART TWO
THE WATERING

Time, the ever soothing Healer, marched forward with his sturdy, unyielding strides, the heel prints of his Yesterdays partially erased by the erosive rains and winds of Today; yet, with unswerving confidence, he went into the Tomorrows and tomorrows and tomorrows.

The Sun Goddess, daughter of Time, looked down with benign grace upon her jaded jewel, set in the blueness of the Pacific Ocean. Amidst the green fields, native farmers engaged in unending cultivation of the sweet potato, which, for hundreds of years has constituted the staple diet of the people of Okinawa. Here and there, among the toiling workers, small groups were removing the coral rock and rubble of bomb destruction in order to rework the soil more effectively for present and future plantings.

Off-shore, The United States Army Transport, "Marine Hurdler," rode leisurely at anchor preparing the discharge of her civilian passengers; employees of the Army Corps of Engineers, assigned for purposes of reconstruction on the island for the Occupation Forces.

The transport lay in the outer harbor. Docking facilities were not available. Air bombings, sea barrages and the subsequent bitter land fighting had rendered unloading docks and piers useless. Consequently, the men were to be discharged over the side into two L. C. I.s (landing craft, infantry) which plied their way back and forth from ship to shore like busy water bugs. The creaking and groaning of the winches unloading baggage and the scraping of the L. C. I.s as they rubbed alongside the larger vessel were the only sounds that broke the calm of the otherwise shipless sea.

The scene provided a vivid contrast to the days, not too far remote, when countless ships of all sizes and descriptions crowded the waters of The East China Sea, while anxious men waited, keyed and expectant for the order which would send them hurtling toward the beaches. On this occasion, however, all the passengers lolled about on the decks, fished from the fan-tail, and otherwise occupied their time curiously watching the Japanese prisoner of war crews adroitly maneuver the L. C. I.s into position prior to disembarking the unconcerned civilians.

Overhead the skies were a virginal blue. A brilliant hot sun poured its torrid heat down upon the ship only to have its insufferable rays neutralized by the cooling breezes that wafted gently from the direction of the shore. White, billowy clouds of goose-feathery texture floated lazily to starboard while afar in the heavens, a solitary B-29 thundered its way toward its assigned destination. Okinawa was at peace.

Major Robert Haskell, Corps of Chaplains, United States Army, paced the deck of "The Marine Hurdler", oblivious to the bustling activities aboard the transport.

Engrossed in the reading of his breviary, he paused now and again to gaze toward the island with a quizzical air of studied intent.

He resumed his reading. . . . "At that time while the crowds were pressing upon Jesus to hear the Word of God, He was standing by Lake Genesareth. And He saw two boats moored by the lake, but the fishermen had gotten out of them and were washing their nets. And getting into one of the boats, the one that was Simon's, He asked him to put out a little from the land. And sitting down, He began to teach the crowds from the boat. But when He had ceased speaking, He said to Simon, 'Put out into the deep and lower your nets for a catch.' And Simon answered and said to Him, 'Master, THE WHOLE NIGHT through we have toiled and have taken NOTHING; But at Thy Word I will lower the net'."

Father Haskell's trained and practiced eye took in the similarity of the comparable picture looming before him. He saw the two small L. C. I.s bobbing on the waves. He saw the tangling fishing lines hanging over the side of the vessel. Acutely cognizant of his Christ-like vocation, he felt oppressed by a deep-rooted feeling of futile and powerless inadequacy.

With a sudden, decisive movement, Father Haskell abruptly

closed the book. He quickened his pace along the well scrubbed deck of the huge ship. He walked with the nervous uncertain gait of a deeply agitated man. He turned quickly to move toward the steel rail of the soldier-laden transport, drawn magnetically by a forceful inner compulsion distressfully disturbing to his usual equanimity. Sweat rolled from his perspiring face, now a deep shaded red induced by the feverish fervor which beset him. Gripping the rail to steady his trembling legs, he mopped his pulsating brow as he minutely studied every aspect and feature of the nearby shoreline.

A solicitous G.I., who had been silently watching the distraught actions of his chaplain, stepped swiftly to his side. "Don't you feel well, Chaplain?" he asked.

Father Haskell placed his hand upon the shoulder of his young charge. "I'm all right, Son," he replied. "Thank you." Calm and relaxed now, he pointed in the direction of the island. "Take a good look at that island, Son," he said. "You stand here, safe and secure on this ship because thousands of others like you made it possible to do so. I'm thinking of one in particular, whom I knew quite well."

"Yes," he went on reminiscently, "it seems as though it were only yesterday that I first met him. It was in November, 1941, that I interviewed a youngster for entrance into the seminary. His qualifications and desires fitted him admirably for the arduous life of a missionary, spreading The Word of God. However, with the declaration of IVA, he felt that his place was on the firing line and he answered his country's call to action. I heard from him frequently." The chaplain paused chokingly. "One day there were no more letters. That boy's destiny was Okinawa; dropped like a tiny mustard seed on the fertile soil of a pagan land."

The young soldier bowed his head. and stood speechless in the presence of .the heartbreak he knew possessed the soul of this sincere soldier of God and Country.

After a moment the chaplain resumed. "For some inexplicable reason, since we anchored here this morning, he has been so constantly in my thoughts that I've had an irresistible urge to go ashore—but—orders are orders, aren't they, soldier? Our post of duty is Korea!" Opening his breviary, he immediately found his place in the book and moving reluctantly away from the rail, he slowly resumed his patient pacing of the deck.

At long last, the men were loaded aboard the L. C. I.s. Between the calls of farewell from the crew and the unforgettable wartime phrase of "you'll be sorry", ringing in their ears, shouted by the Korean- bound G. I.s who lined the rails to observe the debarkation, the first civilian invasion of Okinawa was under way.

They clambered up the bulwarks of the small craft with an eager expectancy to view the general scene of destruction and chaos, quite unlike their combatant predecessors, inasmuch as no necessity existed to compel them to crouch down, out of a line of fire.

As the vessels approached the shoreline, the first glimpse of the havoc of war became more readily discernible. Fire-gutted and hull-punctured ships of various tonnages, both American and Japanese, cluttered the harbor, some lying on their sides and others with stern or bow sticking up out of the water, victims of the relentless Kamikaze suicide planes, naval and air bombardments and the disastrous typhoon of 1945. The sight of damaged and useless wreckage was appalling to the eyes of these builders, unaccustomed to theatres of conflict and seeming wastefulness.

The L. C. I.s crunched their way upon the coral rock-strewn beach, the bows creakingly lowered, then struck the ground and quivered lurchingly to a stop. Imbued with an air of curiosity and adventure, the gaping newcomers streamed ashore, suitcases in hand instead of rifles and with the assured fearlessness that accompanies knowledge of absolute security.

The waiting trucks were soon loaded and with a clashing and grinding of gears, the vehicles roared out of the dock area onto the main highway that stretches the length of the island.

Naha, capital and main city of Okinawa with a pre-war population of sixty thousand had suffered almost complete effacement. Mere shells of a few modern type buildings remained, gaunt and depressing, the steel ribs of the reinforcements showing through the shattered holes in the concrete as they stood there like motionless, ghostly creatures of stone and steel. By no concentration of the imagination could anyone conjure a mental picture of the teeming activities which had once coursed through busy city streets, now merely desolated and deserted expanses of confusion-torn destruction.

The absence of native folk and the eerie atmosphere served to act as dampening influences on the occupants of the trucks which rolled through the ruined city, but this mood was soon dispelled by the exuberant greetings of a group of Okinawa kids trudging patiently along the road.

"Ha-wo," they called.

One of the Americans turned to his companions and exclaimed laughingly, "Did ya hear that, fellers. They can't say hello!" All joined in the general hilarity which followed this remark.

As the trucks rolled toward the north, The East China Sea lay on the left and the receding sun in a flaming dance of variegated splendor cast its rays over the water, lighting up patches of golden beaches hiding in the coves, inlets, and indentations of the coast-line. The shadowed greens of the forest growth, the white- capped waves breaking over coral reefs in a turquoise sea, combined in a breathtaking panorama of exquisite oriental beauty. Off-shore, just beyond the breakers, its tail jutting out of the shallows, lay a stricken Japanese fighter plane. Along the beach, amphibious craft (ducks) stood battered and deserted; their period of usefulness apparently ended and the memories of their short voyage retained in the minds and hearts of the men who bravely manned them on that historic April day.

At this point the truck passed a Shinto Arch. There it stood in all the dignity of its age, seemingly unmarked among the ruins, in all the gracefulness of its symmetrical design as though the Gods themselves had ordained its preservation.

"Say, guys," one fellow inquired in a raised voice. "What d'ya call that thing?"

"Search me?" replied another, looking disinterestedly away.

The quiet, evenly modulated voice of a third speaker broke into the conversation, "That's a Shinto Arch, known to the people of this island as The Gateway to Heaven."

"Well, there's no gate there now," wisecracked the first speaker, grinning smugly at the other fellows in the truck.

"There never has been a gate in the manner which one regards any gate that opens and closes," was the quick rejoinder. "The only barrier is a mental barrier. The Gateway To Heaven is always open to all men whose minds are open; whether it's a Shinto Arch; a Christian Church; or a Synagogue."

"Listen to the preacher," one sneered.

"No fellows, I'm not preaching. I'm just repeating what I read aboard ship on the way over."

A few more men leaned over toward the discussion group. "Go ahead, Jack," one prompted, "Tell us more."

Shyly, the speaker launched into his explanatory discourse. "Well," he said, "Okinawans and Japanese practice a religion called Shintoism. The word is formed by two Chinese words Shin—and--Tao; Shin meaning God and Tao meaning Way.

"The Way of The Gods. They believe that the Will of the Emperor is the sole law in defining what is right and what is wrong. Shinto maintains that the Mikado is a direct descendant of Susano, The Sun Goddess, and so he is the ruler by divine right as he is a divinity in humanity. Shinto has associated with it a system of hero worship and attributes spiritual agencies to the powers of Nature. The ethics of Shintoism are compiled in. one rigid law. Obey the Emperor and be true and faithful to the ideals which the conscience of your heart and mind dictates."

"Like all religions, it sounds like a lot of foolishness and superstition to me," a newcomer to the group scoffed.

"Not necessarily," Jack answered. "These people were willing to die for their faith. You, also, may be called on one day to die, not for a faith which you lack, but for the privilege of being able to express your belief or disbelief in whatever other opinions you may hold; economic, political, or religious. Think that over, Mac!"

The group listened intently. The speaker went on. "Some wise guys may call it preaching but mark my words. The PRACTICE of what is preached, by nonbelievers as well as believers, is the only tangible means and the sole solution remaining to Man of insuring his material and spiritual salvation in a world too far advanced in. technical progress to cope with the basic selfishness of his primeval instincts and nature." The speaker halted for a moment and then went on. "These docile people here on Okinawa come closer to a realization of God's purpose without the aid of revealed religion, much the same as did the ancient philosophers, Socrates, for one, who, arrived at the incomplete answer by pure reason alone."

Silence fell upon the group. The motor of the huge truck drowned out the possibility of further conversation as the driver pressed the accelerator to the floor in order to climb over the next incline without shifting gears.

Further up the road, just as the truck poked its nose over the rise, the full view of The Island Command Cemetery came into sight. Situated on a high slope but nestling in the cradled valley of other terraced heights, the rows of pure white crosses and stars of David stood erect in their geometrical alignment. At the masthead of the flagpole, the rippling folds of the Stars and Stripes shimmered full blown in the breeze, spreading its mantle of protection and inviolability over every single marker on the ground below.

Inconspicuously there, among the men he loved, lay the mortal remains of a most famous war correspondent. Had he, instead, been an occupant of the passing truck, more than likely he might have been overheard murmuring half to himself, but directly addressing his fallen comrades, the beautiful lines from "The Lady of the Lake";

"Soldier, rest; thy warfare o'er,

Sleep the sleep that knows not breaking; Dream of battled fields no more, Days of danger, nights of waking" . . .

At the foot of the cemetery hill, an American chapel, its tapering steeple contrasting with the surrounding foreign landscape, outlined its miniature gothic architecture against the exotic sky. It served as a sobering reminder to every man riding in the convoy, that home and all its tender memories lay far behind, back across. the far reaches of the deep Pacific.

Beyond, they witnessed their first fascinating view of the peculiar Okinawan tombs, so famous for the part they played in affording concealment for the Japanese soldiers as the opposing forces bitterly contested for possession of the island. Set into the sides of hills and cliffs, they had the appearance of the back shell of an immense turtle. For the most part they are described as formed in the symbolic shape of a womb, implying that interment represents a normal return to the bosom of Nature, Mother of all mortal things and original source of life.

In the fields, off the road, and dotting the landscape, stood the shattered or burned out shells of American tanks, resting in the craters where they were knocked out of action by high powered enemy explosives. Some showed the gaping hole of the mortal wound which Nature's healing action mercifully sought to hide by causing the lush vegetation to thrust its verdant way through the aperture.

Native women were at work in the fields and the new crop of sweet potatoes blossomed prettily in the yellow hue of its flowers all about the monument-like tanks. Their guns were forever silenced, yet pointing southward as grim reminders of the soul-stirring struggle in which they fought their victorious drive from the original beachhead. Behind the ruined tanks the terrain rose gradually but majestically in a series of foothills cut deep by wide and irregular valleys and leading to a lengthy escarpment, the slashed formation of its ridge resembling the irregular, sharpened edges of a large hacksaw. Heavy woods covered the ridge with curiously shaped table top trees standing forth against the horizon.

The convoy rolled along at an average speed of thirty-five miles an hour over ground which a short time before had been bloodily conquered with the resultant casualties that made the Okinawa campaign the hardest and most bitterly contested in the entire sweep to the north. A few more miles brought the crowded vehicles to their destination in an Army area. The sun had set. The initial detail of transportation was ended.

The hours wore on with the indefatigable sameness so characteristic of all military establishments. Darkness came. The mosquitoes buzzed incessantly. Again the locusts hummed their click-clack melodies. The pungent odor of the Orient, a combination blended of the smell of unfamiliar growths, rain-rotted canvas and of the newness and strangeness of a foreign land made sleep for the newcomers almost impossible. The night wore on.

At taps, plaintive notes from numerous bugles in the various Army installations joined together in exact unison, echoing and re-echoing, their fading strains borne afar by the air currents that swept in coolingly from the sea, eddying throughout the valleys and over the hills. In thatch-roofed villages, weary Okinawans, worn from the day of back-breaking toil in the fields, stirred; comfortable on their sleeping mats and confident that all was well in the camps of the Americans; snuggled closely together and relaxed exhaustedly in the luxury of their security. All too was quiet in the tents in which the newly arrived Americans lay, the rhythmic breathing of some indicating successful somnolence. Finally, silence reigned. Another night had settled its cover on Okinawa.

The sun that had slowly closed its venetian blinds on one side of the world gradually opened them, little by little, distributing its munificent beams down upon The United States of America. The war had ended not so very long ago. But now, everywhere, people busied themselves in the complexities of a modern, industrialized civilization. New problems had arisen to occupy the minds and activities of men. Okinawa became a mere paragraph in the newly-written history books; an insignificant fleeting phase in the global warfare that once had raged all over the entire world.

Now the ever-widening threat of World Communism spread its dark shadow over lands that men had died to free. The disillusionment which invariably follows in the wake of war was somewhat allayed and retarded by the unexpectedly continued prosperity within The United States of a post-war employment covering sixty million Americans; on farms, in the factories, and in the marts of trade.

Demand still exceeded supply. Thoughtful men kept their fingers crossed, hoping that social unrest and volcanic upheaval would not rise up in the face of a sudden, economic collapse. The Great God, Money, was the magical entity at whose shrine most men worshipped; many, because of insatiable greed and the majority, through necessity.

Meanwhile, the perpetual undercurrent of emotion, entirely

strange and foreign to the male mind, flowed on in its silent stream in the hearts of the women all over the world. Millions of women, mothers of those who lay under the carpets of green, like modern Rachels, wept for their children and would not be comforted.

The group of Okinawan kids who had so effusively greeted the truckload of newly arrived Americans along the road that late afternoon had continued on their happy way. They were in no hurry. Laughing, fooling, jostling one another, they gamboled their way upon the highway of their carefree boyhood, pausing now and again to wave a greeting to the occupants of passing Jeeps, Weapon-Carriers, and to the entire steady stream of American motor traffic speeding indifferently by.

Despite the adversities of war-torn dislocation, they reflected the stoic, philosophical attitude of their elders. Reared in an atmosphere of what would be defined by the western world as "abject poverty", they gloried in the possession of over-sized U. S. Army field boots, decrepit fatigue jackets, and trousers issued by Military Government Agencies. Their meandering journey took them away from the city, plodding along the sun-baked road which winds up and down northeastward from Naha to Shun.

Occasionally they wandered off the road into the underbrush, dallying here and there to scan the ground searchingly for empty cartridge shells, which, when found, like typical boys everywhere who treasure inconceivably useless objects, they stuffed into already overloaded pockets. As they trotted back and forth, brushing aside the long blades of clumped grass covering the ground, one of the boys found himself standing on the edge of a depression. The banking suddenly gave way and he slid on his heels, still standing upright into one of the holes which pockmarked the earth in the immediate vicinity, as reminders of the recent hostilities.

His companions laughed at him in gleeful peals of heart-warming humor as he sought to scramble out of his ludicrous predicament. He clutched at the rooted grasses with his left hand as he bounded buoyantly out of the foxhole into which he had fallen. As his groping fingers had combed the earthy sod, he had felt the unfamiliar hardness of the metal object enclosed within the tightness of his clenched fist. Now safe on the upper level again, he scrutinized his find closely with a mixed reaction of curiosity, wonderment, and horrorstricken awe.

Superimposed upon a vertical bar, four inches in length, lay the half-naked figure of a man. His arms were outstretched across a similar bar two inches in length and horizontal to the other. The hands and feet, he found upon closer examination, were transfixed by what appeared to be nails, while just under the ribs on the left side of the body, was an unmistakable wound such as might be caused by a spear or some other closely related weapon. A crown of thorns encircled the head, which hung lifelessly on the right shoulder, chin resting on chest. It was a small, silver crucifix.

Excitedly, he called to his friends who gathered about him to study this exceedingly unorthodox mode of what they readily perceived must be some type of human punishment or execution.

As if in harmony with the slowly setting-sun, the spirits of the boys sunk; crestfallen, and subdued. Gone was the light-hearted gaiety of the afternoon. With a solemn dignity of which they were innocently unaware, they resumed the homeward trek, perplexed as to the nature of The Thing one of them carried, timidly and reverently in the open palm of his hand.

It was dusk when they entered the village, snugly situated in a deep valley, protected from the wrath of Fuujin, God of Wind, who carries the winds in a sack on his back. -When Fuujin opens his bag, the terrible typhoon blows. Beyond the village, typical of all the other villages on the island, lay a panorama of rolling hills, cultivated fields and winding roads. The streets within the village were merely rows between the neat thatched-roof huts. Despite the lateness of the hour, small children and toddlers played in and about the huts, darting here and dashing there in helter-skelter fashion. Mothers carried their babies in the time-worn traditional mode of their folk, the little tykes slung in a hammock- like sash across the mother's back.

Clustered in groups in front of many homes, the older children sat listening to the tales of their elders concerning the days when Okinawa was ruled by a proud and kind monarchy, independent of both China and Japan. Or, the story was related of a prior visit to Okinawa by Americans, when, in 1854, Commodore Perry's tiny fleet, returning from his historic voyage to Japan, stopped off at Naha, leaving six of his valiant crew of American sailors buried under plain stone markers in the well-cared for International

Cemetery. Stories were told too of Adanya, a poor but extremely gracious and generous woman who, one day in prayer to Futema-Gonyen, guardian God of Voyagers, had her prayers answered by a gift to her of jewels and riches. In commemoration of this long ago event, the Shinto Shrine was erected in a cave over five hundred years ago.

The ancient tale was retold, perhaps, of Amani-Kiyo and Shineri-Ko, the Okinawan version of Adam and Eve. It runs thus:

In the beginning, the Gods had provided the couple with sufficient food each day by the simple process of having it drop from the heavens. At first the two of them were content with their daily allowance, but before long the woman began to put aside some food each day for use in the event of a future time in which the food failed to rain. The Gods, apparently, were displeased with this lack of faith in their provision and discontinued the daily shower. Amani-Kiyo and Shineri-Ko were forced to labor; they had to turn to the sea and the fields for their food. So Okinawa became a fishing and agrarian nation.

Then too, there were the stories of the various other Gods; of Daikoku-Ten, God of all the land, who carried in his hand a hammer, symbol of work from which flowed coins to show his followers that the way to riches is through hard work. He always was seated on a bag of grain and over his back he carried a sack of gold—the result of his diligent attention to the soil. They also told of Ju-Rojin, God of Life; of Kaminari, God of Lightning; of Bishaman-Ten, God of War, who for all his ferocious appearance is a righteous god who makes war for only high and honorable ideals. In his left hand he always carried a shareito (Lamp of Righteousness). His right hand a Yari (lance). He wears a Roroi, an armour made of heavy cloth reinforced with metal strips.

In addition to the various stories of the Gods and their ways, the usual folklore tales never failed to hold the wide-eyed interest of the children as they sat, knees drawn up under chin beneath the pale moon of the semi-tropical night.

A favorite of all Okinawans concerned the adventures of Urashima-Taro who departed from Okinawa to return to Japan riding on the back of a friendly Kame sea-turtle and carrying a gift from the Otohinie (Princess) of Okinawa. Urashima-Taro was a young Japanese fisherman who was always kind to sea turtles. As a young man his ship had drifted far southward and was wrecked. The entire crew except Urashima was lost, but a friendly Kame carried him to Okinawa. He was impressed with the beauty and peacefulness of the island and remained for sixty years. His fame as a kind, gentle and honest man had spread throughout Okinawa and won the admiration of the Otohime at Shun. When he departed for Japan he still had the appearance of a young man, though he was eighty years old. The Owhime presented him with a box and told him that as long as he did not open it he would remain young.

When he arrived in Japan, he found all his former acquaintances were old and bent. Finally, out of curiosity, he opened the gift to attempt to learn the secret of eternal youth, but when the box was opened the contents escaped in a puff of smoke—and with the escape of the secret, Urashima-Taro immediately became an old man, wrinkled and bent. He never returned to Okinawa, his island Paradise.

When the storytelling was done, the boys separated, each to his own home. The young Okinawan who had found the Crucifix, slowly approached his hut, minutely studying the form outlined on the cross, vainly striving in his mind to interpret the meaning and purpose behind the significance of such an oddly designed work of art.

Noiselessly removing his shoes before entering; he tiptoed to the side of his sleeping mother, who lay upon a mat on the floor. He nudged her gently. "Mother," he whispered, "Awaken." She looked up drowsily and inquired, "What do you want, Son?"

He proffered the Crucifix. She took it in hand, examined it intently for a moment and a suspicious look of inquiry crossed her face.

"Where did you get this, my son?"

"I found it, Mother, in the woods off the road near Shun i Castle while hunting for war mementoes," he replied. Pressing for the answer he sought, he asked, "What is it, Mother?" She shook her head negatively.

"I do not know," she answered. "But tomorrow you may ask Ta-me. He is old and wise and has traveled far. He will have the answer for you." She gently stroked his gleaming, black head.

"Now, come to bed," she said, "You, too, must be weary after such a long walk from Naha."

He placed the Crucifix on a shelf, undressed, and stretched out on his mat. He was soon breathing deeply in the innocence of his youth, resting comfortably in the arms of The God of Sleep.

The shrill, clarion call of the colorfully plumed fighter cocks, maintained by Okinawan men for amusement and for gambling announced the approach of another day. The purple dawn was breaking with the rim of the sun peeping over the horizon far out in The Pacific. Despite the early hour the entire village was astir. The people moved about in a leisurely and deliberate manner, intent upon their tasks but in the worryless fashion which for countless years had motivated the day to day activities of these simple, shy, content, people.

The morning meal over, whole families departed the village. The women and girls went to work in the fields; younger sisters with their infant brother or sister securely strapped to their backs, trotted alongside, their appointed task being to care for and amuse the infants between nursing periods, which on Okinawa, sometimes continues until a child is three years old. The men and boys trudged along through the patches of sweet potatoes to the rice paddies which stood on the level stretches of terraced hillsides or down in the low marshlands by the sea. Only the very old men remained behind. Years of toil and responsibility, of duty well performed, had earned for them a place in the sun to while away their remaining years in the solitude of ease and retirement.

Ta-me, worldly-wise and learned patriarch of the village of Yonabaru, sat immovable on a small bench outside his hut, where daily he sagely watched his world go by. Time was when Ta-me sailed the seas of the earth; first as a fisherman out of the main fishing settlement of Itoman; later, on larger vessels to Shanghai, Tokyo and still later to Melbourne, San Francisco and all the other busy harbors in both hemispheres whose portals open to the interior of mysteriously interesting foreign lands. Now he casually observed the abashed and timid approach of a youngster, who, he perceived, carried in the outstretched hand, a small metal image which he immediately recognized as being a duplicate of "The Crucified One—God of the Christians".

The boy bowed low before the old man in courteous token of deferential respect. He stood silent. The old man broke the hypnosis of the boy's reticence. Reaching forth, he placed a kindly hand on the younger shoulder and drew him close. "What is it you wish, my son?" he asked.

The child held up the Crucifix. "What might this be, 0 Honorable One?" he inquired. The old man stroked his chin whiskers reflectively before answering, as if determining in his mind how simply he might impart the knowledge he possessed to this eager one who might someday sit in the patriarchal chair.

Finally, he began in a patient knowing voice—"This, my son," he said, "is He whom people of the West call 'The Light of the World.'"

He paused for a moment in contemplated satisfaction of the

explanatory start. He went on. "This just and good God took mortal form in order to teach mankind that all men everywhere in the world are brothers and that they should love and respect one another. He said that there was but One God. That He was the Son of God. Thereupon, those who were not His followers said that He blasphemed, and for this crime, they nailed Him to a cross, like this," and again he tapped pointedly on the Crucifix. "How cruel!" commented the boy. The old man smiled compassionately.

"My son, in every age, in times of conflict and discord, some leaders of men, leaders, mind you, for most men are good of heart, some leaders do cruel things either in ignorance or outright contempt for The Word which 'The Enlightened One' taught."

The boy nodded in understanding. "Do those who speak nightly in the village street of this new force called Communism also believe in this God? They do not believe in our Gods."

"No, my son, and I caution you not to be taken in by their words and promises since they believe in no Gods at all; remember this! Every man must have a God to look up to, even if only a personal one. Avoid the pitfall of Communism." The boy stood erect, studiously absorbing the words of The Wise Man.

The Ancient One went on. "This 'Son of God' whom they call The Christ,' taught that all men are made in the One God's image and likeness and are possessed of an immortal soul.—That all who hear His Word and keep it will live forever. To prove this, He promised that three days after His Death On The Cross, He would rise again, glorious and immortal. Those who believe and faithfully practice His teachings enjoy a calm peace of mind in resignation to His Divine Will. They are called 'Christians'".

"Why then, 0 Ta-me, does this just God permit such terrible suffering as the horrible war which has just lately ended? Is he not a cruel God?"

"No, most inquisitive one," the old man replied. "Sometimes, as we mortal men quail and wince in physical and mental torment, enduring the travail of every day's work and the cruelties of war such as we recently witnessed here on Okinawa, we are forgetful of the women who bear our children. Childbirth is, as you have been taught, a power of Nature; an event whose purpose is to bring a new being into the world. Yet, the love of a mother for her child is increased and her joy made fuller by the realization that through her contribution of pain and anguish, a child is brought into this world. As she suckles her offspring, pressing the tiny one to her breast she never ceases to marvel at the formation of such a wonderful creature. The Christians say that such was The Christ's love for all mankind; that He died in order that all men might live. As in childbirth, my son, with its painful suffering, so too, This God, called 'The Christ,' by His Agony and Death upon the Cross, in the closing moment of His final, physical effort, sighed a great sigh and brought forth 'Immortality.' You ask why there are wars. Our Gods too, have their reasons for wars being fought." The old man rested.

The boy gazed enraptured, looking full into the good, crease-lined face of the aged man.

The boy shook his head wonderingly. Finally, he said, — "Why did you not accept this religion, 0 Wise One?"

The old man sighed and regarded the boy closely.

"All this which I have related," he said, "I read in a book many, many years ago aboard a ship at sea. To believe, in full faith, I need to learn more. I did not inquire further. I never became a Christian." He stopped abruptly. Again stroking the white beard of his chin, he continued; half-indecisively, half-confessedly; "Maybe also, like so many men who might affirm what appears to be a truth, I was too worldly reluctant to express openly, my budding belief, for fear of ridicule."

"But," he paused again, "You are young. Great changes are taking place in the world today. Okinawa is no longer an unknown and forgotten little island. It may be that holy and pious men will come to Okinawa so that they may teach us more about the religion of Him whom they call 'The Light of The World.'"

In a gesture of finality, he reached out and clasped the boy firmly by the shoulder with paternal kindliness. "Now, run along," he said, "I must take my nap in the healing sunshine."

PART THREE
THE BLOOMING

The Imperial Japanese Rescript in which The Mikado renounced all claims of divine origin and descent struck Okinawa and Japan with a devastating impact. The power and destructiveness of improved atom bombs which fell upon Hiroshima and Nagasaki were small in comparison. It shocked men's minds, leaving their physical bodies intact and untouched. All the concepts of an idealistic faith, handed down from generations had been obliterated by the single stroke of a writer's pen.

The new Japanese Constitution granting all men equal rights and freedom of religion was in direct contrast to the militaristic, totalitarian code of unquestioning obedience by which so many Japanese had lived — and died.

Confronted with the undeniable admission of the human mortality of his Emperor, the bewildered and confused mind of our simple peasant boy vacillated. Loyal to the precepts of his honorable forbears, yet bolstered by the wisdom he had received from the venerable sage; with a decisiveness born of the impelling urge within him, the boy withdrew The Crucifix from the small recessed tabernacle where he had secreted it and gazed at The Figure in silent contemplation.

Distinctly, he connected the words of the aged philosopher.

"Since every man must have a God, if only a personal one," he soliloquized, "This shall be my God, The God of Brotherly Love and. Everlasting Life."

Now he recalled the story he had absorbed, when, as a tiny child, he had listened in rapt silence to his mother as she unfolded the tale of ju-Rojin, the God of Life, who stands beneath the pine trees. (Okinawans say the Pines never die). Ju-Rojin carries a scroll in his hand symbolic of Wisdom. The deer of the forest gather under the cooling, protecting branches of the pine tree out of the heat of the broiling sun. Hence, the deer too are emblematic of long life.

Taking The Crucifix, he went out of the hut, making his way through the avenues of the village to where a huge pine tree stood at an intersection where the main road led out of the community to the fields beyond. He climbed the tree. With a short length of stranded hemp, he tied The Crucifix to the centre of a limb which overhung the road below.

There it dangled; twisting and turning in its encompassing benediction. Little children gathered about in the simplicity of child-like curiosity. Eagerly, he repeated the wondrous tale to which, only a few days before, he had listened with amazed fascination at the feet of the wise one.

The story spread throughout the village. The next morning, these plain peasants; farmers and fishermen went about their routine of repetition, quietly content in the nonentity of their place in Life's scheme; as uninterested in the unreeling events of the outside world as they had been in the countless centuries of the past.

On the way to the fields, rice paddies, and fishing boats, the paths converged at the pine tree. The Crucifix was suspended from the branch and twirled slowly in the early, morning breeze.

The One God of All Mankind looked down from the height of The Tree of Life whose sturdy roots were firmly set in the rich soil of this tiny Paradise Garden of the Orient. As the men, women and children passed by, their eyes fixed upon the swaying Cross that a missionary might have carried, they bowed in the customary, humble obeisance, typical of their courtly Eastern mannerisms.

In the small town of Lawrence, Massachusetts, the fading strains of the church organ ebbed away as the stoled and surpliced figure of the priest mounted the steps of the pulpit that early Sunday morning. Like the slanting rays of the sun that angle earthward after a tumultuous storm, the shafts of light streamed through the stained-glass windows of the edifice. The beams fell upon the waiting speaker who stood erect, pausing momentarily in quiet dignity as he opened The Book.

The hushed congregation waited expectantly. In a voice of

soothing clarity he began at the proper time to read. The people listened intently as the familiar Story unfolded. . . . "And when they had done so, they enclosed a great number of fishes, but their nets were breaking. And they beckoned to their comrades in the other boats to come and help them. And they came and filled both the boats so that they began to sink. But when Simon Peter saw this, he fell down at Jesus' feet saying, 'Depart from me, for I am a sinful man, 0 Lord.' For he and all who were with him were amazed at the catch of fish they had made. And so also were James and John, the sons of Zebedee, who were partners with Simon. And Jesus said to Simon, 'Do not be afraid; henceforth thou shalt catch men.' And when they had brought their boats to land, they left all and followed Him." The priest paused and with a note of conclusion, he added, "So ends today's Gospel."

The congregation filed slowly out of the church into the bright freshness of a new morning. A middle-aged but still youthful looking couple passed unnoticed among the now rapidly diverging parishioners. They walked quietly along, bowing here and there to friends and acquaintances. She spoke: "Dad," she said softly, "It's all right now." She paused, a happy half smile of momentary reflection passing over her countenance before continuing, "There in church I had the most comforting feeling and a sense of calmness came over me." He said nothing; merely nodding. His eyes widened somewhat to glance sidelong at her, waiting, hoping expectantly for the words he had prayed would come some day to ease the burden of grief they had both borne so valiantly ever since the day the fateful telegram had arrived.

They sauntered slowly down the avenue of flanking elms whose branches arched the now deserted street. Birds twittered and trilled in the needle-like branches of a solitary Pine tree standing strong and erect among the towering elms. With a strangely comforting sense of supreme happiness, he looked straight ahead down the avenue and through a vista of the companionable years that stretched before them.

As they came abreast of the pine tree, he pressed her hand. Instinctively, she edged closer to him. Looking up full into his face, her head nodding in assent as if in confirmation of her thoughts, she smiled, openly, happily, her face lighting with a glowing radiance as she murmured softly, "HE WOULD HAVE BEEN ONE HELL OF A MISSIONARY, WOULDN'T HE DAD."

THE LEGEND OF THE PINE

In the backyard corner of a home at the foot of a hillside street in Methuen, Massachusetts; its steel runners rusted and worn, steering wheel missing, its once sturdy pine planks warped and split by sun and wind, snow and rain; practically obscured by weedy growths and deeply imbedded in the weather tamped earth, stands an old, abandoned bobsled.

Over the top of the hill, on the site of where once "a haunted house" stood useless and deserted, a modern hospital; soon to be staffed by The Sisters of Bon Secours; rises in the process of construction; in the name of The Holy Family.

Non-sectarian in its scope of extending "good help" to ailing mankind, the hospital shall stand as a permanent memorial to the peoples of varied creeds and denominations who so generously contributed an amount in excess of one million dollars to The Archbishop Richard J. Cushing Charity Fund in order to make its construction possible.

A statue of St. Joseph, Patron Saint of Construction Men, stands in a tiny cubicle which is firmly attached to a pine tree whose lofty spire reaches ever skyward. Upon completion of the hospital, the aged, the infirm, and the sick may look down from the height of Mt. St. Joseph over the expansive landscape to soul-stirring scenes of breathless beauty and serenity; to scenes where once, lost boyhoods strutted their fleeting hour; down to where a small pond glistens like a jewel turning in the sunlight; to scenes of twisting paths through the woodland now grown over with health restoring pine trees.

In the waning portion of a summer's afternoon, convalescent patients may observe three small boys lounging on the shore's edge. Not in imagination, but in reality, for Boyhood, like Immortality, is eternal.

Perhaps, though, in that borderland of semi-consciousness that lies between illness and recovery, when, in the stillness of night, fever increases; the imaginary far away cries of "kiss her, kiss her", will reverberate over the rolling hills and through the consecrated corridors of Bon Secours Hospital as a kindly nun hastens to reassure her delirious patient like a mother soothes a fretful child.

Maybe you too, shall never pass a pine tree wherever you or it may be, without imagining that beneath its sheltering shade and climbing through its branches are the transparent figures of Boyhood; some dressed in cowboy and Indian suits, chaps and fringe complete; others in smart military dress or battle-smeared combat gear, retelling their tales of victorious adventure, and still others garbed in old patched trousers such as we ourselves were clad in those dim past, happy days, long ago.

EPILOGUE

This story was written with the intention that the incorporation of the changeless Gospel (God's-story) within the framework of a modern, fictional tale is comparable to exhibiting an ancient masterpiece in a present-day gallery on a small side street and to prove that the Scriptures are adaptable to today's scene just as they have been through the ages and that "Christianity, instead of becoming decadent, is vitally alive and resurgent" . . . (quotation from address of His Excellency, Most Reverend Richard J. Cushing, Archbishop of Boston on November 30, 1948 at the consecration of two new bishops of The Society Of The Divine Word at Techny, Illinois.)

To present a comparative contrast between the elements of Good and Evil, represented in the story by Light and Darkness; to dramatically prove the psychological benefits to be derived from the Word of God which is The Light that dispels all fears of darkness and perplexity.

The purpose of the tale of The Japanese Man and his voyage on the back of the sea turtle is to point out the fact that he remained youthful until the moment he opened the gift which had preserved him from the decrepitude of old age.

The gift is symbolic of "The True Faith"; so long as one does not harass one's mind in endlessly endeavoring to penetrate its unfathomable secret; he remains eternally young at heart. To break open and destroy the "Gift of Faith"; like the character in the story is to become old and bent; wearily burdened with the worries of this world and, alone and unaided, to follow the path or road of disillusionment and unspiritual death.

The Marine character, alone in the foxhole with his faith in God, is comparable to the simplicity of the people of the village as they humbly and respectfully file past The Crucifix on their way to their monotonous, yet necessary toil.

The cover photo is symbolic of the three unnamed characters whose fate crosses paths in that lonely foxhole. Our would be missionary protagonist, the Japanese soldier he attempts to take prisoner, and the young boy whose subsequent fall into that hole leads to the spread of Christianity on the Island and beyond.

The depiction of life on Okinawa, before and after the war, calm, serene, enduring, is to point up the comparison in which Okinawa is symbolic of the world as it might be; the war itself as representing the turmoil and indecision of the world today, as we know it, and to show how The Word Of God, if heeded by our civilization of indifferent men, might re-achieve the tranquility such as existed in The Garden of Eden and the Paradise-like island of Okinawa.

Finally, to serve as an inspiration to those who absorb the story in its entirety to draw their own contrasting inferences, as individuals; an achievement so wide-spreading, like the ripples on a pond as to render the humble efforts of the author, woefully meager and inept by final symbolical comparison.

ABOUT THE AUTHOR

Peter A. Hewett (1908 – 1992) was born and raised in the city he cherished, "The Immigrant City", Lawrence, Massachusetts. Married to Marie Francis McNamara Hewett, they were blessed with four children, Mary, Eleanor, Peter Jr., and Ann Marie.

Peter was the oldest of ten children. Mr. Hewett's mother was widowed when he was 17 years old, leaving Peter to help her raise his nine siblings, a responsibility in which he took great pride. He held a number of positions, including mill worker, laborer, salesman, construction worker, grocery store clerk, and automobile assembly line worker, His work history culminated in a profession he loved, serving for several terms as secretary (the equivalent of Chief of Staff) to Lawrence's Mayor, John J. Buckley. Mr. Hewett retired in the mid 70's and spent his remaining years devoted to his first love – his family and friends and to his second love – reading and writing.

It was during his time and experiences as a civilian construction electrician working with the Navy Sea-Bees in 1946, building up the infrastructure for the United States Military on the Island of Okinawa that the inspiration for A Seed Falls on Okinawa was first conceived.

Mr. Hewett was very much a self educated man. He was a voracious reader who was blessed with the gift of near total recall. A prolific writer of short stories, he was well known to the editors and readers of the Lawrence Evening Tribune for his op-ed and opinion articles. He was active in local civic and religious organizations and was a recipient of a Freedoms Foundation Award for his writing and civic participation. He was beloved by his large extended family of which he was the patriarch.

It is his son's assessment that the essence of his Dad's character is well captured in the poem his Dad insisted that he commit to memory as a young boy.

ABOU BEN ADEHM
by James Henry Leigh Hunt.

Abou Ben Adhem (may his tribe increase!)
Awoke one night from a deep dream of peace,
And saw, within the moonlight in his room,
Making it rich, and like a lily in bloom,
An angel writing in a book of gold:—
Exceeding peace had made Ben Adhem bold,
And to the Presence in the room he said
"What writest thou?"—The vision raised its head,
And with a look made of all sweet accord,
Answered; "The names of those who love the Lord."
"And is mine one?" said Abou. "Nay, not so,"
Replied the angel. Abou spoke more low,
But cheerily still, and said "I pray thee, then,
Write me as one that loves his fellow men."
The angel wrote, and vanished. The next night
It came again with a great wakening light,
And showed the names whom love of God had blessed,
And lo! Ben Adhem's name led all the rest.

That same essence of the man, the author, is also reflected in the beauty and beautiful simplicity of his novella -- "A Seed Falls on Okinawa".